Squid and Octopus

Friends for Always

tao nyeu

Dial Books for Young Readers an imprint of Penguin Group (USA) Inc.

For Yao

DIAL BOOKS FOR YOUNG READERS

division of Penguin Young Readers Group • Published by The Penguin Group
Penguin Group (USA) Inc., 375 Hudson Street, New York, NY 10014, U.S.A.
Penguin Group (Canada), 90 Eglinton Avenue East, Suite 700, Toronto, Ontario,
Canada M4P 2Y3 (a division of Pearson Penguin Canada Inc.) • Penguin Books Ltd, 80 Strand,
London WC2R 0RL, England • Penguin Ireland, 25 St. Stephen's Green, Dublin 2, Ireland (a division of Penguin
Books Ltd) • Penguin Group (Australia), 250 Camberwell Road, Camberwell, Victoria 3124, Australia (a division of Pearson Australia Group Pty Ltd) •
Penguin Books India Pvt Ltd, 11 Community Centre, Panchsheel Park, New Delhi - 110 017, India • Penguin Group (NZ), 67 Apollo Drive, Rosedale,
Auckland 0632, New Zealand (a division of Pearson New Zealand Ltd) • Penguin Books (South Africa) (Pty) Ltd, 24 Sturdee Avenue, Rosebank,
Johannesburg 2196, South Africa • Penguin Books Ltd, Registered Offices: 80 Strand, London WC2R 0RL, England

The publisher does not have any control over and does not assume any responsibility for author or third-party websites or their content.

Designed by Lily Malcom • Text set in ITC Stone Informal Medium • Manufactured in China on acid-free paper • 10 9 8 7 6 5 4 3 2 1

Library of Congress Cataloging-in-Publication Data
Nyeu, Tao.
  Squid and Octopus : friends for always / Tao Nyeu.
    p. cm.
Summary: Four separate stories celebrate the many-legged friendship between Squid and Octopus as they
disagree over how to stay warm, encourage each other, and fret over the contents of a fortune cookie.
ISBN 978-0-8037-3565-1 (hardcover)
      [1. Best friends—Fiction. 2. Friendship—Fiction. 3. Squids—Fiction. 4. Octopuses—Fiction.] I. Title.
          PZ7.N992Sqi 2012
            [E]—dc23
              2011033194

The artwork was silkscreened
using water-based ink and a
colored pencil.

Presenting . . .

The
Quarrel

The Dream

The Hat

The
Fortune Cookie

The Quarrel

One chilly day, Squid knit eight beautiful
socks. They were cozy and warm. He could
not wait to show Octopus.

"Octopus! Come out and see my new socks!" he said.

"Silly Squid," said Octopus. "Don't you know we wear mittens?"

"No we don't. We wear socks," said Squid with a frown.

"Mittens!" said Octopus with a stomp.

"Socks!" said Squid with a double stomp.

They decided that Wise Old Turtle could settle their quarrel.

"Wise Old Turtle, do we wear socks or mittens when it's chilly?" asked Squid.

"Nonsense," said Wise Old Turtle. "When it's chilly, we wear scarves
and earmuffs."

Squid studied Octopus's mittens.

"Your mittens are nice," he finally admitted.

"Those are great socks," said Octopus.

"Should we . . . share?" asked Squid.

A splendid exchange of socks and mittens followed.

"Silly Turtle," said Octopus. "Who ever heard of wearing scarves and earmuffs? Obviously, what we really need is a hot pot of tea."
"And cake," added Squid.

Octopus and Squid cozied up in their socks and mittens.
They sipped hot tea. They munched on cake. They were warm.

The Dream

Octopus was swimming about when he came
across a very droopy Squid.
"Why so glum, Squid?" asked Octopus.
"I just had the most fantastic dream," said Squid.
"I dreamt that I could fly."

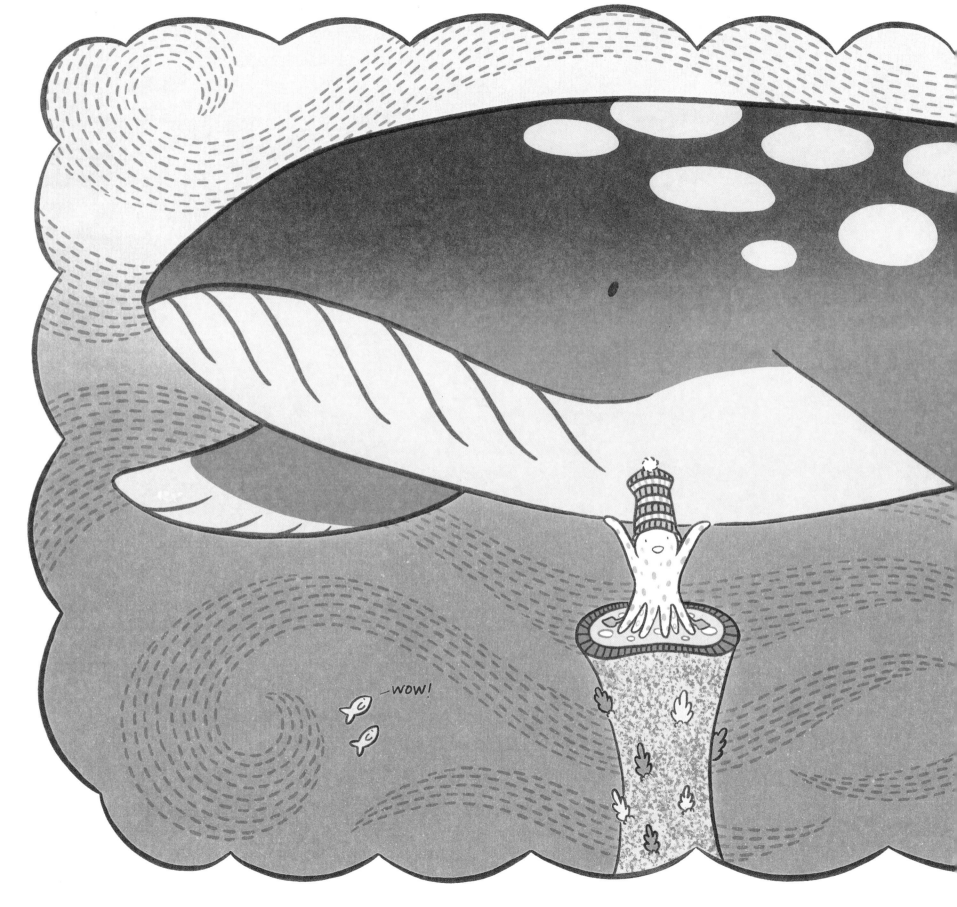

"I dreamt that I had X-ray vision."

X-RAY VISION!
NOW WOULDN'T
THAT BE GRAND?

— GRAND INDEED.

"I was a Super Squid," said Squid.
"Now I am just regular old me again.
I feel so . . . so ordinary."

"Ordinary?" Octopus exclaimed. "Who knit cozies for Hermit Crab's whole family when they lost their shells?"
"I did," said Squid.

"Who organizes Tickle Monday each week?" asked Octopus.
"I do," said Squid.

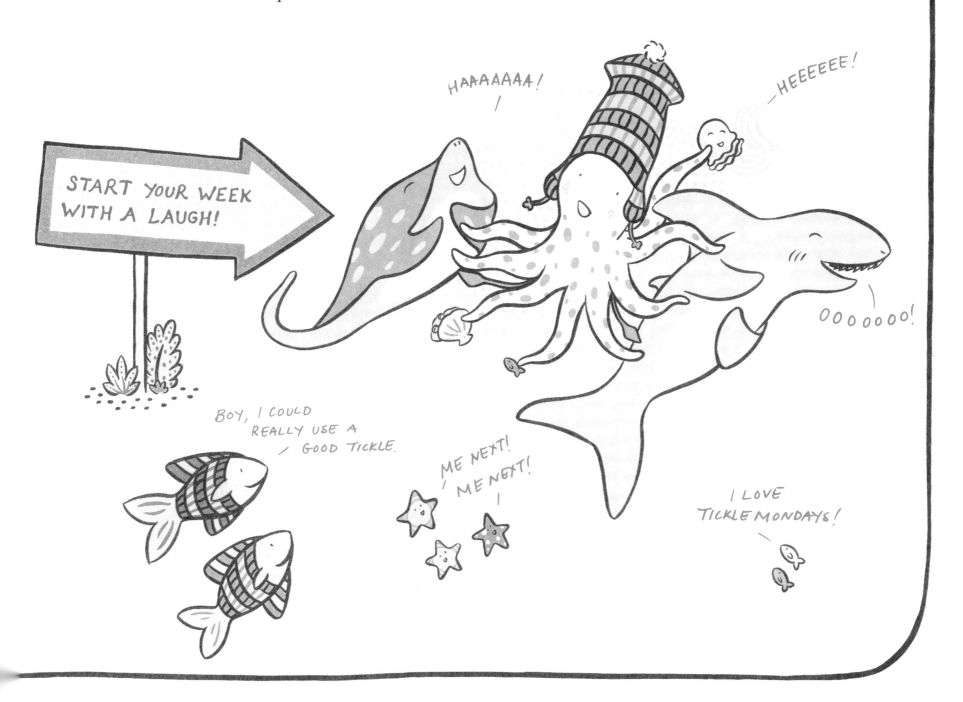

"And who can play all of my favorite tunes
at the same time?" asked Octopus.
"I can," said Squid.

"Well, any squid who can do all that
is a Super Squid!" declared Octopus.

Squid suddenly felt super from head to tentacle. He gave
Octopus his very best hug. It was incredibly strong.

The Hat

Octopus was hard at work when something floated down from above.

"What a fine hat," said Octopus. "This must be my lucky day."

He went swimming along and soon ran into Carl.

"Odd to wear a flowerpot on your head, don't you think?" Carl said.

"A flowerpot? Oh my, I thought it was a hat," said Octopus.

"Thanks for the tip."

He went off to fill his flowerpot.

Octopus was feeling quite pleased with his new flowerpot
when he ran into Margot.

"A soup bowl full of flowers? You're so funny, Octopus," she said.

"A soup bowl? I don't believe it!" said Octopus. "Well, I do feel a little hungry.
What perfect timing."

He went to Yum Yum's, the delicious soup stand.

Octopus was enjoying his soup when Arnold sat down.
"That is a beautiful doorstop, but why are you eating soup out of it?"

"A doorstop?!" wailed Octopus. He felt completely ridiculous.

Back at his home, he put the doorstop in its place. He studied it.
It just didn't feel right.
At that moment Squid burst in through the open door.

"Look at the great hat I found!" Squid said excitedly.
"It *is* an extraordinary hat! I like your style," said Octopus.
He put on his matching hat and the two friends set out for a swim.

They made a fabulous pair.

The Fortune Cookie

"I have a fortune cookie!" said Squid.

"Oooooh," said Octopus. "How exciting. Are you nervous?"

"Why would I be nervous?" asked Squid.

"Well, the fortune could be good or the fortune could be bad," said Octopus. "Until you break the cookie open, there is no way of knowing."

LOBSTER ALWAYS GETS TO BE THE MODEL.

IT'S CALLED A MUSE.

"You are right, Octopus. Look, I have goose bumps. What would a good fortune say?" asked Squid.

"It might say something like 'Among the lucky, you are the chosen one,'" said Octopus.

"I like that," said Squid.

"What would a bad fortune say?" asked Squid.

"A bad fortune could say 'You will have a close encounter of a serious kind.' My goodness, did you just squirt ink on me?"

"Sorry," said Squid. "That fortune was really scary."

"And don't forget the third kind of fortune," said Octopus. "The tricky fortune. Imagine one that said 'Everything is coming your way.' It could be good *or* bad."

"The suspense is too much! Octopus, please open it for me!" said Squid.
"But then it will become my fortune!" said Octopus.
"Could we open it together?" asked Squid.
"Okay," said Octopus. "On the count of three. One . . . two . . . three!"

Together Octopus and Squid cracked open the cookie.

The fortune floated out.

It read:

TRUE FRIENDS ARE FRIENDS FOR ALWAYS.

"Oh, that is a very good fortune," said Squid.

Octopus agreed.

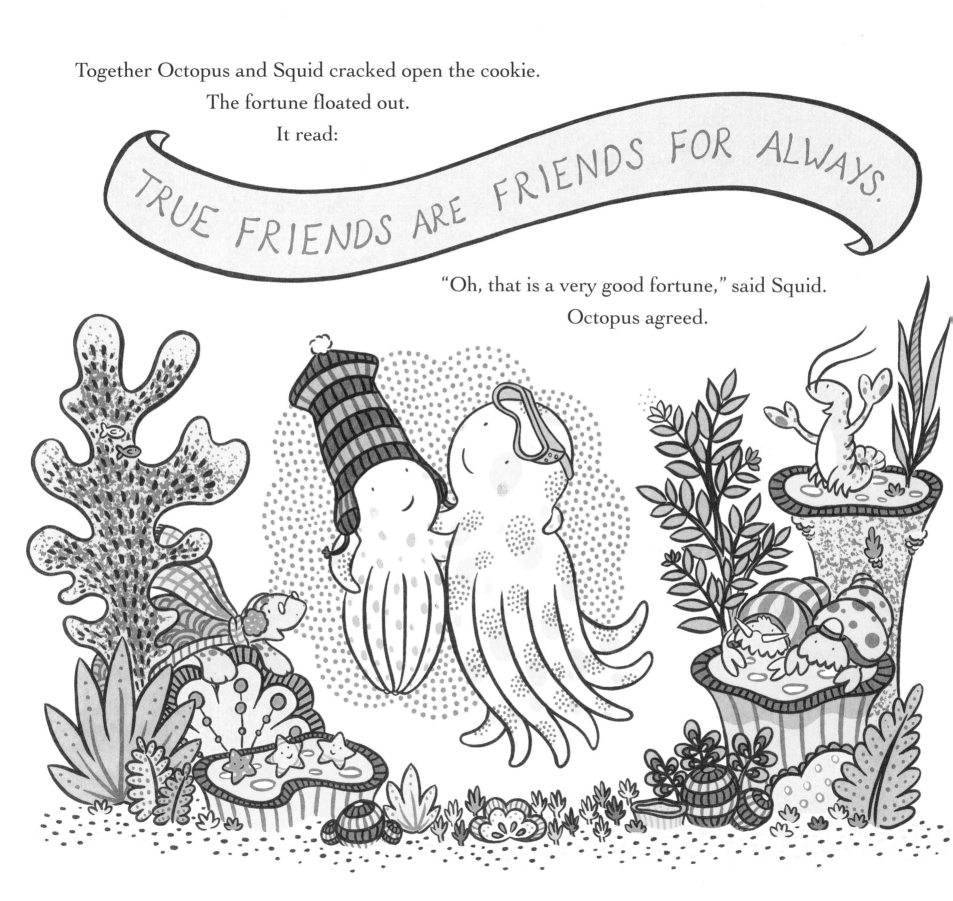